Manufacturing

Tatiana Tomljanovic

Weigl

CALGARY
www.weigl.com

Published by Weigl Educational Publishers Limited
6325 10 Street SE
Calgary, Alberta T2H 2Z9

Library of Congress Cataloging-in-Publication Data

Tomljanovic, Tatiana
    Manufacturing / Tatiana Tomljanovic.
(Linking Canadian Communities)
Includes index.
ISBN 978-1-55388-381-4 (bound)
ISBN 978-1-55388-382-1 (pbk.)
    1. Manufacturing industries--Canada--Juvenile literature.
2. Manufacturing industries--Economic aspects--Canada--Juvenile literature. 3. Manufacturing industries--Canada--History--Juvenile literature. I. Title. II. Series.
HD9734.C22T64 2007   j338.0971   C2007-902246-4

Printed in the United States of America
1 2 3 4 5 6 7 8 9 11 10 09 08 07

Editor
Heather C. Hudak
Design
Warren Clark

We acknowledge the financial support of the Government of Canada through the Book Publishing Industry Development Program (BPIDP) for our publishing activities.

Contents

What is a Community?

A community is a place where people live, work, and play together. There are large and small communities.

Small communities are also called rural communities. There is plenty of open space. Small communities have fewer people and less traffic than large communities.

Large communities are called towns or cities. These are urban communities. They have taller buildings and more cars, stores, and people than rural communities.

Canada has many types of communities. Some have forests for logging. Others have farms. There are also fishing, energy, **manufacturing**, and mining communities.

Types of Canadian Communities

FARMING COMMUNITIES
- use the land to grow crops, such as wheat, barley, canola, fruits, and vegetables
- some raise livestock, such as cattle, sheep, and pigs

ENERGY COMMUNITIES
- found near energy sources, such as water, natural gas, oil, coal, and uranium
- have **natural resources**
- provide power for homes and businesses

FISHING COMMUNITIES
- found along Canada's 202,080 kilometres of coastline
- fishers catch fish, lobster, shrimp, and other underwater life

Real Canadian Communities

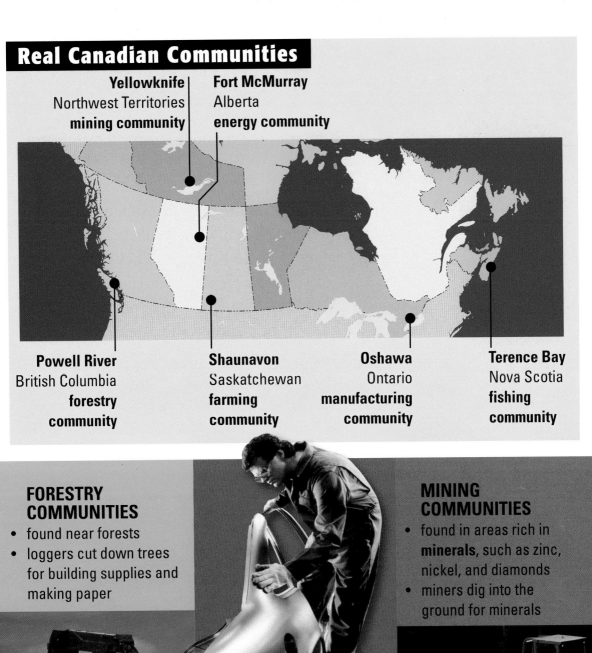

Yellowknife
Northwest Territories
mining community

Fort McMurray
Alberta
energy community

Powell River
British Columbia
forestry community

Shaunavon
Saskatchewan
farming community

Oshawa
Ontario
manufacturing community

Terence Bay
Nova Scotia
fishing community

FORESTRY COMMUNITIES
- found near forests
- loggers cut down trees for building supplies and making paper

MINING COMMUNITIES
- found in areas rich in **minerals**, such as zinc, nickel, and diamonds
- miners dig into the ground for minerals

MANUFACTURING COMMUNITIES
- use natural resources to make a finished product
- finished products include cars and computers

Welcome to a Manufacturing Community

Oshawa, Ontario, is a manufacturing community. It is also an urban community. There is huge plant in Oshawa. Cars and trucks are made there. People in Oshawa depend on the automobile industry. More than 25,000 people work at the plant.

Long ago, people rode in carriages. They were pulled by horses. A company in Oshawa made carriages. Robert McLaughlin started the company in 1876. Then, people began driving cars. Robert turned the carriage factory into an automobile plant. Today, the plant makes cars, trucks, and other **vehicles**.

There are more than 32,000 jobs in the manufacturing industry in Oshawa.

First-hand Account

Ontario

Oshawa

My name is Vince. I live in Oshawa. It's on the northern edge of Lake Ontario. Most of my friends' parents help build cars and trucks at the auto plant. My mom works in the offices at the plant. My dad works in Toronto. It's not too far from home. He takes the train to work each day in Toronto. My family took the train one day to visit the Hockey Hall of Fame.

I play hockey in the winter and lacrosse in the spring. On summer holidays, my friends and I skateboard. There is a skateboard park near my house. During the school year, I go to school six days a week. I have regular school during the week. On Saturdays, I go to Italian school with my brothers. My mom and dad speak Italian to us at home.

Think About It

Compare Oshawa to your community.
- **How is it the same?**
- **How is it different?**

The Manufacturing Industry

Some factories use **raw materials** to make a finished product. Other companies design or sell the finished product. Together, all of these businesses make up the manufacturing industry.

The manufacturing industry is important to many places in Canada. It is also important to industries that collect raw materials. These are farming, fishing, forestry, mining, and energy industries.

—

People make sure machines are working properly.

Timeline

1700s
Canada's manufacturing industry begins with flour mills.

1867
Henry Seth Taylor builds Canada's first automobile in Stanstead, Quebec.

1871
The Canadian Manufacturers' Association is formed.

Manufacturing provides many jobs for Canadians. People work in the auto plant building cars. Not all the people who work at the auto plant make cars. Doctors, nurses, and firefighters also work for the plant. Many workers provide services for other workers.

Machines help manufacture goods faster and cheaper.

1920
About 600,000 Canadians work in manufacturing.

2003
Canada makes 2,552,862 vehicles.

2006
The auto industry is Canada's largest manufacturing industry.

Building Cars

Cars and trucks are important in Canada. Canada is a huge country with a small population. In rural areas, people often live many kilometres from their nearest neighbour. Sometimes, they live more than 10 kilometres from the nearest town. If people had to walk from place to place, it might take them two or three hours to go to school or to the store.

Auto plants, in places such as Oshawa, provide a needed service. They make cars. For many years, cars were built on an **assembly line**. Auto plants have changed. Now, they use new machines and new ways to make vehicles. Assembly lines are being replaced by workstations. Here, people work together. Robots also do many of the jobs that people once did.

Canada produced more than 2.5 million cars in 2006.

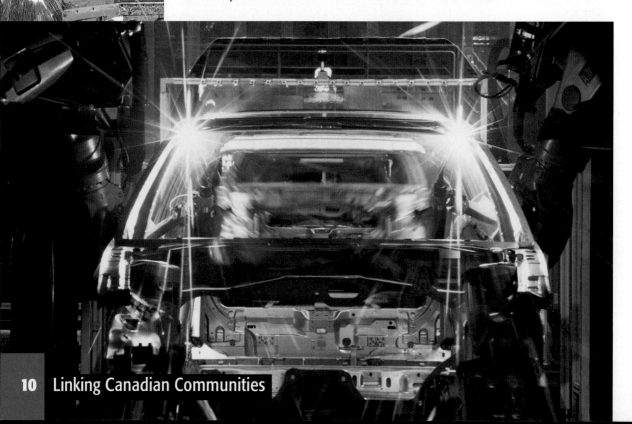

Car Building Process

Car is designed.

Sheets of steel are cut and shaped, based on the design, into parts for the car.

Robots put the car together.

Machines and people paint the car.

People install the engines and the tires.

The car is cleaned.

People check the car for safety.

The car is ready to be sent to stores.

Canada's Manufacturing Map

People use manufactured goods every day. Clothing, food, windows, and cars are manufactured. There are many types of manufacturing industries. The main manufacturing industries in Canada are machinery, clothing, wood and paper, food and drink, metal and mineral, and energy. The auto industry is part of the machinery industry. This map shows some of the manufacturing communities in Canada.

Legend

- Food and beverage
- Clothing
- Wood and wood products
- Machinery and electrical
- Metal
- Rubber, plastics, petroleum, coal, and chemicals
- Non-metal minerals

Iqaluit

Labrador Sea

Hudson Bay

Manitoba

Newfoundland
and Labrador

Ontario

Quebec

St.
John's

Winnipeg

Prince Edward
Island

New
Brunswick

Quebec City

Fredericton

Charlottetown

Nova Scotia

Ottawa

Halifax

Toronto

Atlantic Ocean

Careers

More than two million people work in the Canadian manufacturing industry. There are many kinds of jobs in manufacturing. Some of the jobs include mechanical engineers, motor vehicle assemblers, and truck drivers.

Mechanical engineers research, design, and develop machines. Many work in the auto industry. Some design cars. Motor vehicle assemblers put the car together. They work in auto plants. Then, truck drivers load cars onto specially designed trucks. They deliver the cars to **dealerships** across Canada. Salespeople at dealerships sell the cars.

Computer technology is used to help design cars.

The manufacturing industry needs other businesses to supply services. This makes even more jobs. Plants, such as the Oshawa auto plant, are huge. Oshawa's auto plant has more staff members than some small towns have people. These large plants need many of the same public services that towns need. The Oshawa auto plant has its own fire department, bank, ambulances, doctors, and stores.

Women work in the auto industry as salespeople, engineers, designers, and mechanics.

Some mechanics check automobile brakes and change the oil.

Think About It
What other jobs might there be in the manufacturing industry?

Links Between Communities

Everyone is part of a community. It may be a village, a town, or a city. Communities are linked to one another. Each Canadian community uses goods that link it to other communities. Goods are things people grow, make, or gather to use or sell.

A forestry community makes lumber for construction. The wood may be shipped to another community to build houses or furniture.

Energy communities produce natural gas, oil, and other types of energy, such as wind, solar, and hydro. Other communities use this energy to power their homes and vehicles.

Dairy products and meats come from farming communities that raise cattle and other animals. People in all communities drink milk products and eat meat from these communities. Many farming communities grow crops such as wheat. Wheat is used to make bread and pastries.

These goods may be fish, grains, cars, and paper products. Communities depend on one another for goods and services. A service is useful work that is done to meet the needs of others. People are linked when they use the goods and services provided by others.

Manufacturing communities make products such as cars and trucks. They also make airplanes, ships, and trains that are used to transport, or move, people and goods from one place to another. Transportation services help communities build links.

Fishing communities send fish to stores to be bought by people in other places. In Canada, most fish is caught off the Pacific or Atlantic coast. People living on farms or in cities across the country buy the fish at stores.

Diamonds, gold, and potash can be mined. These items are sent from mining communities to other parts of the country. A diamond might be set in a ring for a person in another community.

Think About It

In your community, what goods and services help take care of your family's needs and wants?

The Environment and the Community

Manufacturing plants produce air pollution called **greenhouse gases**. These gases damage the environment. Greenhouse gases make Earth warmer. When Earth becomes warmer, the **glaciers** melt. This harms the environment. Carbon dioxide is a greenhouse gas. In 2000, the manufacturing industry made 16 percent of Canada's carbon dioxide **emissions**.

Automobile exhaust contains carbon dioxide.

Think About It
How can you help reduce the amount of greenhouse gases your family produces?

Cars, trucks, trains, and ships made by manufacturing plants all have **exhaust**. The exhaust from these vehicles adds to greenhouse gases. Vehicles are a big source of greenhouse gases.

Vehicles need a source of fuel to run. Most vehicles run on fossil fuels. These include gas and oil. Once fossil fuels are used, they are gone forever. Scientists and researchers are looking for renewable sources of energy.

Eco-friendly Fuel

Scientists have been working to make environmentally friendly cars. They would run on hydrogen. Hydrogen is a gas. It can be made from renewable resources. Hydrogen combines with **oxygen** to make water. This mixture makes energy. Hydrogen-powered cars use hydrogen as fuel. They make water instead of exhaust. Hydrogen cars are too costly for most people to buy. Scientists are trying to make cheaper hydrogen cars. There are more than 500 hydrogen-powered cars in use around the world.

Brain Teasers

Test your knowledge by trying to answer these brain teasers.

Q *What do mechanical engineers do?*

A Mechanical engineers research, design, and develop machinery.

Q *Name three types of communities in Canada.*

A Canada has forestry communities, farming communities, fishing communities, energy communities, mining communities, and manufacturing communities.

Q *What two things link communities?*

A Goods and services link different communities together.

Q *Name three types of manufacturing industries.*

A Machinery, clothing, wood and paper, food and drink, metal and mineral, and energy are all manufacturing industries.

Q *Where is Oshawa?*

A Oshawa is located in Ontario.

Q *What is the difference between a rural and urban community?*

A A rural community has plenty of open space and few people. An urban community has taller buildings and more cars, stores, and people.

Make a Model Truck

Trucks deliver manufactured goods across Canada. The manufacturing industry needs trucks and truck drivers. You can build your own model truck by following these instructions.

Materials

- 2 recycled boxes (a shoebox and a smaller, cardboard box)
- poster paint
- different colours of construction paper
- scissors
- glue
- felt markers or crayons
- old newspaper

Procedure

1. Cover your work area with newspaper.
2. Paint the boxes whatever colour you want your truck to be.
3. Once the paint has dried, glue the smaller box on top of the shoebox. This forms the cab of the truck.
4. Cut out construction paper to make wheels, headlights, a driver, and other truck parts.
5. Glue the parts onto the truck.
6. Decorate your truck with felt markers or crayons. Your truck is now ready to deliver goods!

Further Research

Many books and websites provide information on manufacturing communities. To learn more about manufacturing communities, borrow books from the library, or surf the Internet.

Books

Most libraries have computers that connect to a database for researching information. If you input a key word, you will be provided with a list of books in the library that contain information on that topic. Non-fiction books are arranged numerically, using their call number. Fiction books are organized alphabetically by the author's last name.

Websites

The World Wide Web is also a good source of information. Reliable websites usually include government sites, educational sites, and online encyclopedias.

Learn more about the city of Oshawa by visiting **www.oshawa.ca**.

Find out when the Oshawa auto plant opened or what cars and trucks the factory makes by visiting General Motors' website at **www.gm.com/company/corp_info**. Click on "Global Operations," "North America," "Canada," and then the "Oshawa Car Assembly Plant."

Words to Know

assembly line: a group of workers who each do some work on a product and then pass it down the line until the product is completed

dealerships: stores that sell cars and trucks

emissions: gases that come from manufacturing plants and automobiles

exhaust: smoke or gas from an engine

glaciers: slow moving masses of ice

greenhouse gases: the air pollution created by the burning of fossil fuels

manufacturing: making a large amount of something using machines

minerals: inorganic substances that are obtained through mining

natural resources: materials found in nature, such as water, soil, and forests, that can be used by people

oxygen: a colourless, odourless gas that is found in the air

raw materials: products that have not yet been made into something else

vehicles: machines that people use to move around, such as cars, trucks, buses, or bicycles

Index